← YOU CH... P9-DNW-302

SCOOBY-DOO!

THE MYSTERY OF THE AZTEC TOMB

Stone Arch Books
A Capstone Imprint

You Choose Stories: Scooby-Doo
is published by Stone Arch Books,
A Capstone Imprint
1710 Roe Crest Drive
North Mankato, Minnesota 56003
www.capstonepub.com

CAPS31133

Cataloging-in-Publication Data is available on the
Library of Congress website.
ISBN: 978-1-4342-9127-1 [Library Hardcover]
ISBN: 978-1-4342-9128-8 [Paperback]
ISBN: 978-1-4965-0106-6 [eBook PDF]

Summary: Scooby-Doo and the gang are asked to find
out what's behind a haunted archeology site in Mexico.

Printed and bound in China.
003042

SCOOBY-DOO!

THE MYSTERY OF THE AZTEC TOMB

written by
Laurie S. Sutton

illustrated by
Scott Neely

THE MYSTERY INC. GANG!

SCOOBY-DOO

SKILLS: Loyal; super snout
BIO: This happy-go-lucky hound avoids scary situations at all costs, but he'll do anything for a Scooby Snack!

SHAGGY ROGERS

SKILLS: Lucky; healthy appetite
BIO: This laid-back dude would rather look for grub than search for clues, but he usually finds both!

FRED JONES, JR.

SKILLS: Athletic; charming
BIO: The leader and oldest member of the gang. He's a good sport—and good at them, too!

DAPHNE BLAKE

SKILLS: Brains; beauty
BIO: As a sixteen-year-old fashion queen, Daphne solves her mysteries in style.

VELMA DINKLEY

SKILLS: Clever; highly intelligent
BIO: Although she's the youngest member of Mystery Inc., Velma's an old pro at catching crooks.

YOU CHOOSE

SCOOBY-DOO!

Something is scaring the workers at an archeological dig in Mexico. Only YOU can help Scooby-Doo and the Mystery Inc. gang get to the bottom of it.

Follow the directions at the bottom of each page. The choices YOU make will change the outcome of the story. After you finish one path, go back and read the others for more Scooby-Doo adventures!

YOU CHOOSE the path to solve...

THE MYSTERY OF THE AZTEC TOMB

The bright green Mystery Machine bounces along a dirt road deep in the jungles of Mexico.

"Are you sure this is the way to the dig?" Fred asks as the van hits a rough bump.

"This is the only road on the map," Daphne replies. She holds a piece of paper with a few lines drawn on it. "Not that Professor Dinkley sent us much of a map. Velma, your uncle might be a famous archaeologist, but he's not great at directions."

"Like, remind me why we're going to an archeological dig in the middle of nowhere?" Shaggy moans. He and Scooby-Doo munch on Scooby Snacks in the back of the van.

Turn the page.

"Because Uncle Cosmo needs our help solving a mystery!" Velma says enthusiastically. "He wants us to investigate what's scaring his workers away from the dig site."

"Ris it a ronster?" Scooby shivers.

"A monster? Why didn't anyone tell me that before we drove to a spooky Aztec pyramid deep in the jungle?" Shaggy yelps and points ahead.

"We're here!" Daphne says with relief.

The Mystery Machine stops in front of a stone structure covered with vines and small trees. There are shovels and buckets scattered around the pyramid, but there are no people.

"Where is everyone?" Fred wonders as he and the gang climb out of the van. "Hello! Is anyone here? Professor Dinkley?"

"Heelllp!" a faint voice cries.

The gang follows the sound to a heap of rubble at the foot of the pyramid.

"Someone is trapped under those stones!" Daphne realizes. They dig with shovels and their bare hands until they finally see one of the workers. As soon as he is free from the rocks, he tries to run away!

"Wait! Where did everyone go?" Fred asks as he snags the worker's sleeve.

"El Chupacabra! Xolotl! The god brings the devil dogs!" the man babbles and tears away from Fred's grasp. The worker runs down the road until he is out of sight.

"Revil rogs?" Scooby gulps. He looks around nervously.

"What's a cup-a-barbra?" Shaggy asks.

"Chu-pa-ca-bra," Velma corrects Shaggy. "It's the dog monster of Mexico."

Turn the page.

"Zoinks! I knew a monster had to be involved!" Shaggy says, alarmed. He wraps his arms around his pal Scooby-Doo. Their teeth chatter in fear.

"Hey, I found something," Fred announces. He leans into an opening in the pyramid. "When the wall fell on the worker, it exposed this doorway."

"It's a clue! Maybe it will lead us to Uncle Cosmo," Velma suggests. She starts to step into the opening.

"Wait!" Daphne interrupts. She pulls a flashlight out of her purse. "We might need this."

One by one the gang steps into the dark, ancient pyramid.

"Be careful. This place is probably full of traps," Velma warns.

The flashlight lights up a fearsome face!

"Yaaa! A dog monster!" Shaggy shrieks.

"Don't worry, it's just a carving," Velma assures her friends. Daphne is curious and reaches out to touch the stone face. As soon as she does, the floor opens under their feet. They fall!

"Jeepers! A trapdoor!" Daphne exclaims.

The friends tumble down a sloping shaft. Below them, the tunnel splits into several branches.

"Stay together! Don't split up!" Fred shouts. He grabs Velma's hand.

Shaggy and Scooby clutch each other. Velma reaches for Daphne, but misses! Daphne disappears down a branching tunnel. Fred and Velma slide down a separate shaft. Shaggy and Scooby roll into a third chute.

"Ruh-roh," Scooby-Doo gulps.

To follow Shaggy and Scooby into a spooky cave, turn to page 12.

To follow Daphne into an ancient tomb, turn to page 14.

To follow Fred and Velma to an underground city, turn to page 16.

Shaggy and Scooby-Doo pop out of the shaft, clutching onto each other in a ball. They bounce and roll along the stone floor.

BONK! They hit a stalagmite. They bounce off the rock and hit another stalagmite.

BING! They bounce off several more stalagmites until they untangle from each other and flop to a stop.

"Whoa! Like, watch out for that first step, Scoob! It's a doozey," Shaggy says as his eyes roll around in their sockets.

"Reah, rat's a roozey!" Scooby agrees.

They are so dizzy, they think they see stars. Actually, it's the light of tiny candles burning. There's just enough light to see that they are in a small cave, and it's filled with skulls!

"Yaaa!" Shaggy and Scooby shriek.

They run—or try to run! The floor is covered with dried bones that act like rollers under their spinning feet. They trip and fall, face-first, in front of the face of a snarling dog.

"It's the chupacabra!" Shaggy yells.

"Rope, rit's a rock!" Scooby realizes.

The dog turns out to be a carving in the stalagmite. When they look around at their surroundings, they see that they are in some kind of underground graveyard. It's spooky, but not scary—until they are confronted by a glowing ghostly figure with a dog's head!

"I am Xolotl, god of the dead!" it moans. "The living are not allowed here. Prepare to die!"

Xolotl reaches out to grab Shaggy and Scooby.

If Xolotl captures them, turn to page 45.
If Shaggy and Scooby escape, turn to page 49.

Daphne tumbles out of the shaft and into a small, dark room. She rolls a short distance until she bumps up against something hard. Daphne still has her flashlight, and she swings it around. Carved stone faces grimace back at her.

"Jeepers! More creepy carvings!" Daphne exclaims. The sound of her voice echoes off the walls.

Startled, she scrambles backward, almost dropping the flashlight. Her back hits a solid stone wall.

"Wherever I am, it sure is a tight fit," Daphne says as the flashlight reveals a small chamber.

Slowly she realizes that she's in a burial chamber and that the carvings are on a stone tomb! "A sarcophagus!" Daphne shouts to no one.

It's bad enough that Daphne is in a dark, underground tomb with a sarcophagus, but the lid is open!

"Oh, that is not a good sign," Daphne moans.

Curious, but cautious, Daphne slowly shines the flashlight into the sarcophagus and peers inside.

"I'm almost afraid to look," she says.

The stone coffin is empty.

"Well, that's a relief!" Daphne sighs. "I was afraid there was going to be a mummy. Or a vampire!"

Then she notices scratches on the inside of the sarcophagus. With a shudder, Daphne wonders if the person was buried alive and was clawing to get out!

Turn to page 17.

Fred and Velma slide down the dark chute as fast as if it were a waterslide. They finally pop out in a large cave. Even more surprising is that there are buildings inside the cave! An underground city!

"The architecture is ancient Aztec, from before the conquistadors arrived. What a discovery!" Velma says.

"Um, weren't the Aztecs bloodthirsty?" Fred worries.

"Those Aztecs are long gone. Besides, the city looks abandoned," Velma assures him.

She hurries toward the nearest structure and runs her hands across some painted carvings on the side of the building. "Look how fresh the pigment is! The conditions in the cave must have preserved it," Velma remarks.

But Fred isn't looking at the decorations. His eyes are fixed on something more alarming!

"We're not alone down here!" he gulps.

If a snake monster haunts the city, turn to page 35.
If Fred sees dead people, turn to page 89.

"Now, Daphne, stop thinking such wild thoughts!" Daphne scolds herself as she forces down her active imagination. "I have to concentrate on finding a way out of here!"

She looks around as best she can with her flashlight. The beam glints off of something shiny on the floor. It's a piece of gold. Daphne reaches down and picks up a golden cuff. There is a jeweled earring nearby.

"Now I get it. The coffin is open and empty because robbers have been here and stolen treasure from the tomb," Daphne realizes. She brightens with hope. "If they found a way in, I can find a way out."

If Daphne discovers a second chamber, turn to page **22**.
If Daphne accidentally triggers a booby trap, turn to page **63**.

Shaggy and Scooby float into a huge cave. A modern town is built inside the cavern. They climb out of the stream and investigate.

"Like, maybe we can find something to eat!" Shaggy suggests. "All that danger made me work up an appetite."

"Reah! I want a ramburger and a rizza and a rot dog," Scooby slurps.

"I want that, too, with a side of—" Shaggy starts.

HONK! HONK! A truck blows its horn at them! They leap aside and stumble into a café.

SNIFF! SNIFF! "Something smells good!" Shaggy says.

"Hey, you!" a voice demands.

They turn around to see that the customers are all staring at them. A big brute stands up and looms over them.

"You don't belong here," he growls.

Shaggy and Scooby start to shake. The brute points a finger at them.

"You should be working. Now get going!" he says.

Shaggy and Scooby sprint from the café. They hop onto the back of a passing truck. It takes them to a huge staging area. There are cargo trucks being loaded with crates. A crane lowers a stack of crates toward the truck Shaggy and Scooby are in. They are forced to jump out or be crushed.

"Where are we?" Shaggy wonders.

"Shaaaggy! Scooby-Doooo!" a faint voice calls.

"Zoinks! The place is haunted!" Shaggy shudders.

"Look up!" the voice says.

They do, and they see the gang and Professor Dinkley in a cage suspended from a crane!

"Oh, hi guys!" Shaggy says.

Turn the page.

"Get us down!" Fred says.

Shaggy and Scooby go to the crane and lower their friends to the ground. The gang jumps out of the cage.

"Xolotl captured us! But we watched this whole operation from up there," Velma says. "It's an animal smuggling ring!"

"Let's get out of here and call the police," Daphne suggests.

"You aren't going anywhere, you meddling kids!" a voice says.

It's Xolotl! The god of death is back, and this time he's backed by a pack of chupacabras. The beasts snarl and bark. Scooby growls back. The chupacabras bark at Scooby and he barks back. Suddenly Scooby looks surprised.

"Roh, really?" he says.

The chupacabras nod. Scooby leaps straight at Xolotl!

Turn to page 36.

Daphne searches around the tomb with the flashlight. She is thrilled and hopeful when she sees an opening in the wall of the tomb. It looks like a doorway widened by modern tools.

"This must be where the tomb raiders went!" Daphne realizes.

Daphne rushes through the opening—and screams! There are skeletons on the floor of the second chamber! They hold golden Aztec treasure in their bony hands.

"Oh, no! It's the tomb robbers!" Daphne chokes. "They never found a way out!"

They died here, Daphne realizes, and so could she.

Daphne looks around desperately for a way to escape. She sees another opening, but it's small.

"Jeepers, maybe I should lay off the lattes!" Daphne says as she squeezes through the tight gap.

Daphne enters another chamber. This one holds a tiny stone coffin. It's open, and its contents are scattered all over the room. Daphne sees the mummy of a small dog.

"This must have been the pet of whoever was buried in the main tomb," Daphne says. She kneels down beside the little mummy. "I'm sorry that the tomb raiders wrecked your grave."

She collects some of its belongings—a carved stone food bowl and a couple of toys—and places them beside the mummy.

She hears a mournful whimper echo through the chamber.

Turn to page 26.

Scooby and Shaggy enjoy their "lazy-river" ride through the underground tunnels until a speedboat nearly runs over them! Then another, and another!

"Like, we're in the middle of a high-speed boat race. Underground!" Shaggy realizes.

Suddenly Shaggy gets snagged on one of the boats and is dragged through the water like an out-of-control water skier. Scooby tries to doggie paddle out of the way but gets caught by his collar and is flipped into another boat. He lands next to the driver.

"Hurroh," Scooby greets the driver with a big grin.

The distracted driver hits the wake of the boat in front of him and loses control. He and Scooby fly out of the speedboat!

"YaaAAAhh!" they yell as they soar through the air.

The boat driver splashes into the water while the empty speedboat crashes against the wall of the tunnel and explodes.

Scooby lands in the boat dragging Shaggy. Scooby grins at the driver.

"Hurroh," Scooby says then pushes the driver overboard. Scooby grabs the wheel and starts steering the boat—badly. He's a lousy driver.

"Slow down, Scoob!" Shaggy blubbers as he bounces through the water behind the boat.

But Scooby can only go one speed—fast!

The speedboat races along with the rest of the pack until they come out of the narrow tunnels and into a large underground lake.

Turn to page 58.

Shivering from the sound of the sad whimper, Daphne searches, but she can't find a way out of this chamber, either. The flashlight starts to weaken. It flickers ominously, making scary shadows.

Daphne is afraid that there's no way out of the tomb. After all, the robbers died looking for one.

"Velma warned us about booby traps," Daphne remembers. "The thieves must have tripped something that trapped them, and now me, too!"

Daphne sinks to the floor in despair.

"Help!" she whimpers.

Suddenly Daphne hears the sound of a dog barking! She leaps to her feet and follows the sound.

The sound leads Daphne back to the main burial chamber, but now her flashlight goes out. It's completely dark, and Daphne is frightened. She's underground in an ancient Aztec grave with no way out!

"Help! Help!" Daphne calls out. Her voice bounces back at her. "It's no use. No one can hear me. I'm too far underground."

Then Daphne hears scratching sounds. Is that the mummy's ghost clawing to get out of his sarcophagus?

"Yip, yip!" comes a noise like the bark of a small dog.

"Scooby-Doo, is that you?" Daphne wonders.

If Daphne sees an Aztec ghost, turn to page 32.
If the barking is coming from El Chupacabra, turn to page 39.

"Danger! Danger!" an echoing voice bounces off the walls of the room. Fred and Velma jump in alarm!

"I've got a plan. Let's get out of here!" Fred says.

They run out of the building and smack into a group of zombie Aztec warriors! The zombies grab Fred and Velma. As Velma struggles to escape, she kicks her captor in the shin. The creature howls and lets go of her to rub its leg.

"That's one walking dead guy who's going to have a limp!" Velma says.

Fred uses a judo toss to flip his zombie attacker over his head. He yells to Velma, "It's time for Plan B!"

"What's Plan B?" Velma asks.

"It's just like Plan A. Run! Only faster!" Fred shouts.

Fred and Velma run inside a building to hide. This one is crowded with giant clay pots with lids. Fred looks around nervously.

"Are there any mummies in here?" Fred asks.

"No mummies, just zombies!" Velma reminds him. "I can hear them coming closer! We've got to hide!"

"Quick! Get inside the pots!" Fred says.

They lift the lids of a couple of random pots and jump inside. But there's something inside the pot with Fred!

"Augh! There's a mummy in here!" Fred shrieks.

"Augh! Where?!" a voice shrieks back. Arms and legs wrap around Fred inside the giant clay pot.

Turn the page.

The pot tips over and breaks open. That's when Fred sees Shaggy next to him.

"That was you inside the pot, not a mummy," Fred says, relieved. So is Shaggy.

"Like, are we glad to see you! We were being chased by zombies!" Shaggy says.

"Rit was rary!" Scooby says as he pops up out of one of the pots.

Suddenly, zombie warriors burst into the room. Fred and Shaggy jump into different pots to escape. The zombies open the lids and look inside, but that's when Scooby and Velma pop up and smack the zombies on the head with dried maize cobs. When zombies turn to see who hit them, Fred and Shaggy pop up and smack them from behind!

Turn to page 85.

An Aztec ghost appears in front of Daphne in the dark! He is in full warrior garb and wears a feathered headdress. He holds a small dog in his arms.

"Yip! Yip!" the dog barks at Daphne and wags its tail.

"I must be seeing things!" Daphne decides. "This can't be real. After all, the tomb is pitch black—I shouldn't be seeing anything at all!"

But the dog jumps down out of the man's arms and runs over to Daphne. It sits at her feet and lolls its tongue and wags its tail. Daphne reaches down and touches its head.

Her hand goes through the dog like mist!

Daphne snatches back her hand. Her fingers are as cold as ice!

"Yip! Yip!" the little dog barks and trots away into the dark.

"Well, that was weird!" Daphne declares as she watches it disappear.

"Yip! Yip!" comes a bark from the dark. The dog returns to Daphne and yips again. She realizes that it wants her to follow.

"Okay, Lassie," Daphne says and walks after the dog.

It leads her to a wall of the tomb. There are paintings on the wall. The little dog jumps up and pounces against a picture of a dog, which glows in the dark. In fact, it's the only light in the chamber.

"It's a clue!" Daphne realizes. "Good dog!"

Turn the page.

Daphne reaches out and touches the picture on the wall. A doorway opens up! She sees a tunnel with daylight shining at the end of it.

"It's a way out!" Daphne realizes. She turns to thank the little dog, but it's gone.

Daphne runs down the tunnel toward the light. Soon she's out of the pyramid and standing in the jungle.

"What do you know, I'm not far from the dig site!" Daphne says with relief.

Daphne sees the rest of the gang gathered near the Mystery Machine. She waves at them and they wave back. Daphne takes one last look back at the exit, but it's not there!

Just like the dog, it's gone.

THE END

Fred points to a giant snake-like monster weaving toward them. Giant fangs pop out of its mouth, and its face is surrounded by a mane of feathers. Its eyes are red and glowing. Fred and Velma stand frozen in shock, almost hypnotized by the creature. Then the monster turns and heads down a different avenue. Fred and Velma snap out of their daze.

"What was that?" Fred asks.

"Quetzalcoatl! The feathered serpent god of the Aztecs!" Velma gasps.

"First that worker said he saw Xolotl, and now this. Two Aztec gods in one day? There's definitely a mystery here!" Fred declares.

Fred and Velma follow the monster.

If the subterranean city is full of frightful dangers, turn to page 37.

If they are attacked by Aztec warriors, turn to page 47.

Scooby jumps at Xolotl and knocks him down! Xolotl's dog mask goes flying.

"Rhe's a fake!" Scooby says as he sits on the man's chest. "The rittle doggies rold me."

"He looks familiar," Velma says.

"That's because we've met before. I'm C. L. Magnus," the man reveals.

"He's that shipping line owner who robbed his own freighters!" Fred realizes.

"I'm a landlubber now because of you meddling kids!" Magnus says. "I disguised myself as Xolotl to scare off the dig workers and keep them from discovering my underground smuggling operation. And I would have gotten away with it, too, if it hadn't been for your pesky pet dog."

"You solved the mystery, pal!" Shaggy praises Scooby.

The chupacabras gather around Scooby and howl, "Scooby-Dooby-Dooooo!"

THE END

Fred and Velma run after the monster but they can't find it.

"It's gone! Did we imagine it?" Velma wonders.

"No," Fred says and points at some tracks in the dust. They follow the trail, but it leads them around and around until they are completely lost. A tall pyramid looms in the center of the city, and they decide that climbing to the top of it would help them get their bearings. They start to walk down a narrow street, heading in that direction.

"Why are all the walls painted red?" Velma asks.

"You mean, like the color of blood?" Fred gulps.

Suddenly spears rain down on them from the rooftops. The air is filled with the sound of shrieking Aztec warriors. Fred and Velma run for their lives!

Turn the page.

Fred and Velma escape the red street, but now they are in one that's painted blue.

"It's as if the streets are color coded," Velma mutters.

Then they hear a roar. The sound is not human. It's coming from a wall of water rushing toward them! The narrow street is like a canyon funneling the huge wave.

Fred and Velma get swept up and tumble like minnows in a tsunami. The wave crashes and flows down several streets. It comes to a stop at last, but Fred and Velma are trapped in a dead end that fills up like a fish tank. They tread water on the surface, gasping to catch their breath.

"What's next? A big rolling boulder?" Fred sputters.

And then they see the shark.

Turn to page 43.

Daphne gropes through the dark toward the barking sounds. She can't see anything, but she keeps going.

She bumps up against the wall of the tomb. There is a glowing crack that she didn't notice when the flashlight was working.

"This is going to ruin my manicure," Daphne says as she digs with her fingernails.

The crack begins to crumble and widen. Soon she makes a hole large enough to squeeze through. Daphne squirms through the opening and tumbles into a small cave. Her eyes have to adjust to the bright light in the chamber, but when she can see again, she screams!

In front of her is El Chupacabra! And a whole pack of little chupacabras! Daphne has entered their underground lair!

Turn the page.

The chupacabras turn toward Daphne and growl at her. They circle like a pack of wolves surrounding its prey.

"Nice doggies," Daphne says.

She reaches into her purse and pulls out a handful of Scooby Snacks. She throws them at the creatures. They rush in to devour the snacks! Daphne runs around them and escapes out the other side of the cave lair.

Daphne flees down a dim tunnel that opens up into a huge cave. She is stunned to see an Aztec village and pyramid in the center of the cavern. Daphne has only a few moments to think about what she's seeing. Suddenly she hears dogs growling. She knows it's the chupacabra pack. They've eaten all the Scooby Snacks and now they're after her!

Turn to page 42.

Daphne runs through the streets of the underground village. The howling chupacabras are right behind her!

"Help! Help!" Daphne calls out as she twists and turns along the empty avenues of the underground town.

No one comes out to help her. Daphne barely has time to wonder why. She doesn't even have time to knock on a door! She doesn't dare stop!

The pack is faster than Daphne. The chupacabras catch up with their target at last!

"I'm doomed!" Daphne gulps.

The chupacabra pack swarms all over her. They lick her face! They're just a pack of hungry mutts who are happy for the Scooby Snacks and want more!

"Nice doggies!" Daphne laughs with relief.

Turn to page 55.

Suddenly Velma disappears below the surface! Fred thinks the shark has pulled her under. He dives down, determined to save her!

Fred is surprised to see Velma pulling out one of the shark's eyes. **EWWW!** But the eye is mechanical, just like the shark. The machine sinks to the bottom of the tank.

Velma and Fred swim to the surface where they hear clanging alarm bells and lots of shouting. The water drains away as quickly as it filled up. They soon stand high and not so dry next to the broken shark.

A loud voice shouts at them angrily, "You broke my monster!"

Turn the page.

Fred and Velma look up to see a man riding on a boom camera.

"It's a movie! The shark is a prop!" Fred realizes. "Velma, how did you know?"

"A subterranean shark? That only happens in bad movies! That's when I realized the snake and the shark were fake," Velma replies.

"Hey! I know you meddling kids!" the man exclaims.

Velma dries off her glasses and studies him. "I recognize you! You're Carl, the stuntman who wanted to star in Daphne's Uncle Maxwell's movie."

"I'm a director now, and the star of my own movie—*Subterranean Shark*!" Carl says.

"No way! I love monster movies!" Fred gasps.

Fred and Carl walk away in enthusiastic conversation. Velma just rolls her eyes. "Well, that's another mystery solved. But the mystery of movie geeks? That's one I'll never get."

THE END

Xolotl grabs Scooby by the collar and Shaggy by his shirt. He drags them across the subterranean graveyard. Suddenly an elevator door opens! Xolotl drags his captives into the elevator and it descends.

"This Xolotl guy is the god of the dead, and we're heading down. You know what that means, Scoob!" Shaggy moans.

"Reah. Re're doomed!" Scooby whimpers.

The elevator clanks and grinds on cranky gears and finally shudders to a halt. The doors open. Terrified, the pals close their eyes.

"I can't look!" Shaggy says.

"Re neither!" Scooby replies.

Turn the page.

The elevator doors creak open. Scooby and Shaggy fall to their knees in terror. They're too afraid to look where Xolotl has brought them.

"Get up and walk! I refuse to drag you two another step!" Xolotl demands of his captives.

Scooby and Shaggy wobble to their feet. They start walking, but they keep their eyes closed. Shaggy immediately trips over Scooby. They get tangled up in a ball and start to roll. Xolotl chases after them but can't catch up. Shaggy and Scooby are escaping and don't even know it!

If a tiger—yes, a tiger!—thinks Scooby and Shaggy are a ball to play with, turn to page **72.**

If Scooby and Shaggy roll down a mineshaft, turn to page **100.**

The feathered serpent leads Fred and Velma to an Aztec pyramid in the center of the subterranean city. Velma can't help but comment on the architecture.

"Everything looks almost new! It's amazing!" she says.

A door opens up in the pyramid, and the snake monster glides inside. Just as Fred and Velma reach the door, it slams shut. They search, but there's no visible way to open it from the outside. The seams are so tight that no one would ever know a door was even there.

"We've got to get inside the pyramid if we're going to solve this mystery," Velma says.

"Or, maybe we should run," Fred says and points at something behind her!

Turn the page.

Fierce Aztec warriors march toward them with sharp swords raised. Fred starts to flee, but Velma doesn't move.

"Aztecs didn't have metal swords," she mutters.

Fred grabs her by the wrist and they run. Arrows fly past their heads. One embeds itself in a wall next to Velma's face.

"That arrow is tipped with steel. Something's wrong with this picture," Velma observes.

They duck into an open doorway and hide in the shadows as the warriors race past. Velma watches them go, still mulling over the historical mistakes.

"This is weird. Look!" Fred says. The room is full of stacked crates and boxes, spools of cable, and some modern tools.

"The ancient Aztecs didn't have these, either," Velma says.

Turn to page 52.

"Zoinks! It's time to make tracks, Scoob!" Shaggy yelps.

Shaggy and Scooby turn and run! This time they have traction. They race down a dark tunnel. Thick cobwebs threaten to tangle them up like ropes. Their wild rush disturbs a colony of albino bats that flutter around them like a swarm of mosquitoes. And the whole time the glowing ghost of Xolotl follows them!

The tunnel ends when it meets an underground stream. The pals stop at the edge. There's nowhere else to go. Xolotl makes a grab for them, but they jump into the water.

"Geronimo!" Shaggy shouts.

"Scooby-Dooby-Dooo!" Scooby howls.

They splash into the stream and are happy to escape the god of the dead. Until they come face-to-face with albino cave piranhas!

Turn to page 51.

"Zoinks! Man-eating ghost fish!" Shaggy gulps.

Shaggy and Scooby churn their arms and legs like motorboat propellers. They zoom away from the piranhas. They speed downstream and plunge over a small waterfall. Suddenly they are in midair, their legs still spinning.

"Ruh-roh, another roozey!" Scooby says.

They drop a short distance and splash into a calm pool of water. They look around, but there are no piranhas. They are in a wonderland of glowing moss and albino lizards clinging to the walls.

Scooby flattens out like a plank and floats with Shaggy riding on him like a canoe as they drift with the current.

If the stream takes them to an underground town, turn to page 18.

If Shaggy and Scooby drift into a dangerous situation, turn to page 24.

Fred and Velma each grab a heavy tool for protection and cautiously creep out of the building. Velma looks at the architecture with new insight.

"The reason the paint on these buildings looks so fresh is because it *is* fresh. This is new construction," Velma says.

"Who would want to build a subterranean Aztec city?" Fred wonders.

"Xolotl," Velma says and points at the pyramid.

On top of the central pyramid a robed figure lifts his arms high and spins in a strange dance. Their attention is focused on him so they don't notice what's behind them until Velma feels a hand clamp down on her shoulder! She looks down at it. It's not a hand. It's a paw.

"Yaaa! El Chupacabra!" Velma shrieks.

"Yaaa! Where?!" Shaggy yelps as he looks around in terror.

Fred and Velma turn and see the rest of the gang. It was Scooby's paw on Velma's shoulder.

"We've been wandering around the city looking for a way out and haven't found one," Daphne says.

"Well, somebody's found *us*!" Fred says as a group of Aztec warriors surrounds them.

Velma faces the warriors with the heavy wrench in her hands and says bravely, "Take us to your leader."

The gang is marched through the streets to the pyramid. They get into an elevator and ride to the top of the structure. Now Velma knows for certain that the city is new. They exit the elevator and face Xolotl, Aztec god of the dead!

Turn the page.

"Nice city you've got, Xolotl—but that's not who you really are." Velma says.

Xolotl raises his arms and makes growling noises, but Velma doesn't budge. Her friends shiver and tremble, but Velma shakes her wrench at the death god.

"Everything about this place is fake, and so are you!" Velma declares.

She drops the heavy tool on the ground close to Xolotl's feet. He jumps back.

"A god shouldn't be afraid of a little toe bruise," Velma says. "But you aren't a god."

Velma reaches out as quickly as a feathered serpent and snatches the mask off Xolotl's head. Everyone gasps at what they see!

Turn to page 81.

Daphne wanders through the streets of the underground city looking for a way out. The dogs follow her, begging for more Scooby Snacks. She sees a large crowd around the pyramid.

"That's where everyone is!" Daphne realizes.

They're watching an Aztec priest perform a crazy dance on top of the structure. Shaggy and Scooby are up there too, and they're tied up!

Daphne runs toward the pyramid. The pack follows her. Strangely, the people barely move when they see the chupacabras. It's like they're sleep walking.

Daphne scrambles up the steep steps to save her friends. She reaches the top just as the Aztec priest finishes his strange dance.

Turn the page.

Daphne knocks the priest away from Shaggy and Scooby. He loses his balance and tumbles over the side of the pyramid.

"Are we glad to see you!" Shaggy says as Daphne unties them. "That Xolotl guy was about to put a curse on us!"

They look down at the priest lying at the bottom of the pyramid. His headdress is shattered. The crowd wanders around as if coming out of a dream. Among those people are Velma, Fred, and Professor Dinkley.

Daphne, Shaggy and Scooby run down the pyramid to their friends.

"What happened?" Daphne asks them.

"What happened?" they ask in reply.

Suddenly Xolotl jumps to his feet and starts to run!

The chupacabra pack swarms Xolotl and knocks him down. They chomp onto his dog-head mask and tear it off!

"I recognize this guy! It's Harry the Hypnotist!" Daphne says.

"That's right! I used an experimental mind-control device in the headdress to make the villagers think I was the Aztec god, Xolotl. Then I ordered them to mine precious gems and minerals from the caves," Harry confesses. "I didn't want Professor Dinkley to discover the underground operation, so I abducted him and scared off the workers. And I would have gotten away with it, too, if it weren't for you meddling kids!"

"Another mystery solved!" Shaggy says.

"I think this time the credit goes to the dogs!" Daphne laughs as the chupacabras beg for more Scooby Snacks.

THE END

A boat zips past Scooby's speedboat as the
race enters the open waters of the underground
lake. The wake flips Shaggy onto the bow of
Scooby's boat. He stands on the bow like a surfer
riding a wave.

"Hurraaahhh!" a loud cheer goes up.

That's when Shaggy and Scooby see bleachers
full of people watching the race! Shaggy and
Scooby wave at them.

Distracted, Scooby doesn't watch where he's
going and drives the boat off course and onto
the shore. The boat stops, but the pals go flying!
They somersault through the air and land on
their feet.

"Nice form, Scoob!" Shaggy says.

"Rank rou," Scooby replies. Then his eyes go
as wide as dinner plates. "Ruh-roh!"

A pack of chupacabras race toward them!

"Ruparabras!" Scooby yells.

"Relax, Scoob. They're just racing dogs," Shaggy assures his pal. "We landed in the middle of a track. Zoinks! We're in the middle of a track!"

The dogs chase Shaggy and Scooby around the racetrack. As soon as they cross the finish line, a voice comes over a loudspeaker.

"And the winner is Scooby-Doo!" the voice announces.

"Huh? How'd he know your name, Scoob?" Shaggy wonders.

"Ri rust be ramous!" Scooby says.

"I don't think they want your autograph!" Shaggy says and points at a group of armed guards running toward them.

Shaggy and Scooby turn to flee but collide with the robed and masked figure of Xolotl.

"The death god! We're doomed," Shaggy says as the two pals faint!

Turn to page 64.

"We meet again, Harriet Mullins! I see you're still stealing priceless relics," Velma says to the unmasked Xolotl.

"Velma Dinkley? How did you get here?" Harriet replies.

"I asked her and her friends to come solve the mystery of who was scaring off my workers," Professor Dinkley says.

"It looks like that mystery is solved," Fred declares as he unties Daphne and Uncle Cosmo.

"I recognized Jocko from our last encounter. Your own parrot gave you away," Velma says.

"Jocko! Jocko! Gave you away!" the bird says and flaps his wings.

"Stupid bird!" Harriet says and knocks him off her shoulder.

Jocko flutters over to Velma and lands on her shoulder. She pets his feathers and says, "Jocko is a good bird. Aren't you Jocko?"

Turn the page.

"You meddling kids!" Harriet grumbles as Fred ties her hands. "I disguised myself as Xolotl to scare off Cosmo's workers. The subterranean city is filled with treasure, and I didn't want anyone to discover my looting operation. I would have gotten away with it, too, if it hadn't been for that loud-mouthed parrot!"

"Jocko did a great job and deserves a reward. How about a Scooby Snack?" Daphne says.

She holds up a treat, and Jocko, Scooby, and Shaggy all straighten up. Daphne tosses each of them a Scooby Snack. Jocko flaps his feathers and squawks.

"Scooby-Dooby-Doooo!" Jocko says.

Scooby chuckles. He flaps his elbows like wings and repeats, "Scooby-Dooby-Dooo!"

THE END

Daphne searches around the tomb with the flashlight. The walls are painted with the images of the person who was buried here. She notices an attractive piece of jewelry painted on the wall and inlaid with sparkling stones.

"Oh! That's gorgeous!" Daphne says, sighing. She reaches out to touch it. "Um, maybe not. I remember what happened the last time I touched something in this Aztec pyramid. It opened a trapdoor!"

Daphne pulls back her hand and takes a step away from the wall. Just like that, she hears a **CLICK** under her heel.

"Uh oh!" Daphne gasps.

The floor opens and she falls!

If Daphne comes face-to-face with Xolotl, turn to page 71.
If Daphne discovers a treasure chamber, turn to page 91.

Shaggy and Scooby wake up in a room with their hands tied behind their backs. The rest of the gang is there, too, and they're tied up as well.

"At last, you meddling kids of Mystery, Inc. are my captives. Now I can have my revenge," Xolotl gloats.

"Since you know us, you obviously aren't Xolotl. You're a fake, but who are you?" Velma says.

"Why don't you solve the mystery!" Xolotl challenges.

"Well, the pitch of the voice tells me it's a man," Daphne says.

"His accent is American," Fred deduces. "He could be Sam Crenshaw. He found that underground city. We're underground."

"Or it could be Buck Master. He dog-napped Scooby once," Daphne suggests.

"Oh! I bet it's that lawyer, Cosgoode Creeps! He was just . . . creepy," Shaggy says.

Xolotl rips off his mask and throws it to the ground.

"No!" he fumes. "I'm not any of those losers!"

His face is revealed, but no one recognizes him.

"I'm Crocker Pitt, the racecar driver!" he says. "Because of you kids I can't show my face on the official race circuit anymore, so I went underground—literally. The caves under the Aztec pyramid were a perfect place for my racing and gambling ring, until Professor Dinkley started digging."

Suddenly Velma, Daphne, and Fred burst free of their bonds and tackle Pitt!

"You're lousy at tying knots," Fred says and ties up Pitt with his own ropes.

"Guys, a little help? Scooby and I aren't so good at *untying* knots," Shaggy says.

THE END

Fred and Velma run! They crash through the brittle clay wall of the chamber, leaving human-shaped silhouettes. They crash through wall after wall until they suddenly find themselves falling.

They splash into slimy water. The vampire and the chupacabra stare down at Fred and Velma from above, then disappear. As Velma and Fred tread water, they see that the walls of the well are honeycombed with holes and openings of all sizes.

"I've got a plan," Fred says. "We can use those holes as handholds and climb out of here."

They try to climb, but their hands are slimy and the wall is slick with algae. They'll never make it to the top. They're doomed!

But then Fred and Velma reach an opening in the wall and crawl into it.

"It's a tunnel! And there's a light at the end," Velma says.

The slime makes them slip uncontrollably down the tunnel. They pop out into a vampire lair and are immediately surrounded.

"I'll protect you, Velma!" Fred vows. He grabs the nearest object to defend them. It's a bag of potato chips. "Since when do vampires eat potato chips?"

Suddenly a vampire and a chupacabra run into the lair.

"Some tourists fell into the cenote! We've got to help—" he shouts. Then he sees Fred and Velma. "Oh. Never mind."

He plops down into a comfy chair and takes out his fake fangs.

Turn the page.

"You're not vampires. You're a bunch of kids!" Fred gasps in surprise.

"Hey, look who's calling us kids!" one of the vampires laughs and snatches the bag of chips from Fred.

The vampires and the chupacabras break their ring around Fred and Velma. They all plop down in comfy chairs and proceed to ignore their unexpected visitors. Velma looks at their surroundings.

"This is their clubhouse! They're only pretending to be vampires for fun," Velma concludes.

Fred looks closer at their pale faces. "Great makeup, guys! Sorry I didn't realize it sooner. I'm used to seeing masks."

He leans over to Velma and whispers: "What about those chupacabras?"

"I think they're just pets," Velma whispers back.

"Oh, now I get it," Fred says. "These kids are the ones who scared off your Uncle Cosmo's workers. Not cool, guys."

"Hey we didn't mean to! We were just exploring the tunnels down here. Some of them lead to the pyramid," one of the boys explains. That gives Velma an idea.

"You can make it up to Uncle Cosmo by showing him the tunnels and guiding him around the underground city," Velma suggests.

The boys agree.

"Great. Now can one of you show us the way out of here? I need a shower!" Velma says.

THE END

Daphne slides down another chute. It's full of thick, sticky spiderwebs.

"Eww! Eww!" Daphne sputters.

She emerges from the chute covered in spider goo and albino spiders the size of her fist. They crawl in her hair and over her clothes. As Daphne flails her arms and twists her body to get them off, she stumbles out of darkness and into light. Her eyes are dazzled by the sudden brightness. She can't see, but she can hear screaming.

"The Death Monster of Mictlan!" a voice shouts.

Daphne looks around for the monster. She sees a man dressed as an ancient Aztec warrior, wearing a snarling dog mask. Then she sees her friends tied to wooden stakes. They are surrounded by chupacabras!

Turn to page 83.

Shaggy and Scooby clutch each other and bounce like a ball. Suddenly they hear the roar of a giant cat. They feel its paws batting them around like a toy.

The pals hit a bump and untangle. They land in a flop on top of each other. Resting on top of them is a tiger! It looks a little dazed.

"What's a tiger doing in an Aztec pyramid?" Shaggy wonders.

"Ri don't care. Run!" Scooby says.

They run—right into an open cage. The door clangs shut and locks.

"That kitty can't get us now! We're safe!" Shaggy sighs with relief.

But Scooby points to something behind Shaggy and gulps. "Ri don't rink so!"

Shaggy sees that they are in a cave full of stacks of caged animals. There are parrots and monkeys and jungle cats and tanks of tropical fish.

"Is this is a zoo?" Shaggy wonders.

"Shaggy! Scooby!" a voice says. It's coming from the animals in the next cage.

"Like, I didn't know other animals could talk like you, Scoob!" Shaggy says and scratches his head like a confused monkey.

"Re neither!" Scooby replies.

They look at the animals in the cage and realize it's Fred, Daphne, and Velma dressed up in animal costumes!

Turn the page.

"Like, what's with the animal costumes?" Shaggy says.

"It's an animal smuggling ring!" Velma says. "Xolotl dressed us up so no one would know we're human. He plans to ship us out of here. We have to escape!"

The gang shakes the bars of the locked cages. Everyone looks at Daphne, expecting her to save the day. She shrugs.

"I'm sorry! I lost my purse!" Daphne says.

Turn to page 92.

Suddenly Fred catches a glimpse of a shadowy shape race past the door outside.

"What was that?" he yelps.

They hear a flapping sound.

"It's probably just some bats," Velma concludes.

"Not vampire bats, I hope!" Fred shudders.

"Don't worry, Fred. They only drink blood from animals. Hmm, come to think of it, so does El Chupacabra. Its name means 'goat sucker' after all. Maybe there's a connection!" Velma says.

Fred does not look comforted. "Velma, sometimes the less I know the better."

Velma shrugs and they both laugh. Suddenly a hideous face appears in the doorway! It has pale skin and fangs. Standing next to it is a gruesome canine with glowing red eyes.

"Yaaa! A vampire!" Fred shrieks.

"Yaaa! A chupacabra!" Velma yells.

If Fred and Velma flee, turn to page 66.
If the monsters are not what they seem, turn to page 93.

Shaggy and Scooby jump into another forklift and race after the truck.

"Whoaaa! I wish I knew how to drive this thing!" Shaggy says as he knocks over crates and cages.

The cage doors pop open and animals escape. Suddenly the cave is in chaos! Xolotl comes running to see what the commotion is all about.

SCREEECH! The truck carrying the rest of the gang slams on its brakes when confronted by the tiger. Shaggy swerves to avoid hitting the truck and snags Xolotl by his robes. The dog mask flies off Xolotl and lands on Scooby's head!

The forklift crashes to a stop against a cage. Xolotl is tossed into the cage and the door slams shut.

Turn to page 78.

The gang gathers around the caged Xolotl, now revealed to be a man.

"I knew Xolotl had to be a disguise when Shaggy mentioned costumes. But who is this guy? He looks familiar," Velma says.

"I'm Randal Bakko and I wish I'd never met you meddling kids!" the man grumbles.

"You smuggled animals in Africa! You called yourself Randar the Ape Man!" Fred recalls.

"He disguised himself as Xolotl to scare the workers from Uncle Cosmo's dig to keep his smuggling ring a secret," Velma concludes. "Say, where is Uncle Cosmo?"

"Help!" comes a voice from a nearby cage. It's Uncle Cosmo in a gorilla costume. Another gorilla is hugging him. "Would someone please tell this lady gorilla that I'm married?"

THE END

Daphne twirls her purse and flings it at Sammy. ***THWAK!*** It hits him on the chin and he falls down. She shouts a command at the chupacabra dogs and they swarm him.

"Nice throw!" Fred says.

Daphne sets her friends free. Then she bends down and wags a finger at Sammy.

"You are going to show us the way out of this cave or you'll end up as a chupacabra chew toy," Daphne tells him. Scooby-Doo and the chupacabra dogs growl at him.

"Okay! Okay! You're the new goddess in town," Sammy says.

Daphne pats him on the head.

"Good boy," Daphne says with a smile.

THE END

"Gibby Norton!" the gang says in unison.

"Hi, Velma! How do you like my theme park?" Gibby giggles.

"I think you should have studied Aztec history better," Velma replies.

Daphne is annoyed. "Gibby, I know you've had a crush on Velma since you were kids, but will you please stop trying to impress her with these ridiculous schemes?"

"Aw, Daphne, you have no sense of romance! Besides, I've always wanted my own theme park!" Gibby says. He waves his hand as if creating an image in the air. "Can't you see it? Gibbyland!"

"So you dressed up as Xolotl and scared away Uncle Cosmo's workers to attract tourists?" Velma says.

"No, I was just testing out my act, but that's a great idea!" Gibby replies.

Turn the page.

Gibby links arms with Velma and walks toward the pyramid's elevator.

"So, Velma, tell me what I did wrong with the Aztec history! You know I value your opinion!" Gibby says.

Fred and Daphne roll their eyes. The Aztec warriors look confused. "So, are we on a break now?" they wonder.

Shaggy and Scooby peer over the edge of the steep pyramid.

"Like, this would make a great water slide!" Shaggy says.

"Rho reeds water?" Scooby replies.

"I like the way you think, pal!" Shaggy says and grabs a plank of construction plywood. The pals ride it down the side of the pyramid like a surfboard.

"Scooby-Dooby-Dooooo!" they shout.

THE END

"I am Xolotl, god of the Aztecs, ruler of the underworld! Kneel before me!" Xolotl demands as he points at Daphne.

Daphne pays no attention. She is focused on the man's modern wristwatch. Clearly, he's a fake! She takes a closer look at the chupacabras. They are simply small, hairless dogs.

"Sit!" Daphne commands the dogs. They sit obediently.

The crowd is impressed. Daphne decides that two can play this game. She is still covered with cobwebs and albino spiders. She spreads her arms and makes a declaration.

"I am the goddess Daphne! Kneel before me!" she shouts.

The crowd kneels. Daphne turns to Xolotl and snatches the mask off his face.

"Imposter!" she accuses.

The crowd gasps. So does Daphne. She recognizes the man!

Turn the page.

"I know you!" Daphne whispers to Xolotl. "You're Sammy the Shrimp! You robbed an armored car and tried to disguise it as an ice cream truck. Untie my friends or I'll sic the 'chupacabras' on you!"

As Sammy hurries to untie the gang, Daphne faces the crowd.

"I will punish the imposter! You may leave!" Daphne instructs the crowd.

The people walk away obediently. When Daphne turns around, she sees that Sammy hasn't untied anyone.

"You meddling kids ruined my scheme!" Sammy grumbles. "I robbed that armored car to get rich. Then I found this underground village and its gullible inhabitants. I made them think I was a god! I was treated better than a king!"

"Well, you're about to be dethroned," Daphne declares.

Turn to page 79.

The zombies knock over the pots and try to break them. They can't, so they kick the pots, which starts them rolling. The pots roll out the door and down the street then quickly disappear around a corner. The zombies can't catch them!

One zombie smacks another zombie in the back of the head. "Rrr garr murrr!" *(Translation: "Nice move, genius!")*

The other zombie smacks the first zombie. "Gurr arrgh!" *(Translation: "It was your idea!")*

The two zombies start fighting each other. As the other zombies watch the fight, Fred, Velma, Shaggy, and Scooby sneak out of the building and escape.

Turn the page.

"We've got to find Daphne and get out of here," Fred says.

"Find Daphne!" a voice repeats. They look up and see a large green parrot. "Get out of here!" it squawks then flies off.

"I have a theory. Follow that parrot!" Velma says.

They follow the bird to a tall pyramid. The top rises up to a hole in the roof of the cave. A makeshift cargo lift is carrying bundles of treasure out of the cave through the hole. Workers climb up the side of the pyramid carrying sacks of Aztec treasure on their backs. Zombie warriors guard the workers.

"Well, there's our way out. We just have to get past the zombie guards," Velma says.

"I have a plan," Fred declares.

Fred, Velma, Shaggy, and Scooby sneak up behind the guards and overpower them. They take the warriors' uniforms and disguise themselves as guards. The gang walks up the side of the pyramid alongside the workers.

When they reach the top, they see Daphne and Professor Dinkley tied to a stone pillar. Supervising the transfer of treasure is Xolotl! The green parrot sits on his shoulder.

"That treasure belongs in a museum," Dinkley protests.

"Then a museum can pay me for it," Xolotl replies.

"Pay for it! Pay for it!" the parrot squawks.

"Jinkies! I know that voice!" Velma gasps. She races forward in her warrior disguise and pulls the Aztec dog mask off of Xolotl!

Turn to page 61.

"Xolotl!" Velma yelps.

"Yaaa! The death god!" everybody screams. But Daphne puts her hands on her hips and frowns.

"You know, I've been scared by a stone carving too many times in this crazy pyramid," Daphne says, annoyed.

She walks up to the face and raps it with her knuckles. Suddenly a hand grabs her wrist. Now that spooks her!

"Yaaa!" Daphne screams.

"Yaaa!" Fred and Velma scream.

"Yaaa!" Shaggy and Scooby scream. They dive back into the treasure pile to hide.

The mound shudders then collapses like a landslide. A wave of treasure rushes over Fred, Velma, Daphne, and Xolotl and carries them out the door.

Turn to page 98.

"Mummies!" Fred gulps. He stares through a doorway into one of the structures.

"Mummies!" Velma says excitedly and rushes into the building to take a closer look.

The room is filled with Aztec treasure that only an archaeologist could love. There are painted pottery cups and dishes, small statues carved from stone, and walls painted with scenes of the daily life of the person entombed. Everything surrounds a wrapped corpse lying on a stone slab.

"What a fantastic discovery!" Velma gushes. "I wonder if Uncle Cosmo knows about this?"

"Maybe that's why he's missing," Fred speculates.

"You're right, Fred. And if he's in danger, then so are we," Velma concludes.

If Fred and Velma discover that the dead are dangerous, turn to page 28.

If they see a spooky shape, turn to page 75.

Daphne tumbles down another dark chute and lands in a small chamber.

"Velma! Fred! Am I glad to see you!" Daphne says. "Where are Shaggy and Scooby?"

"Right rear!" Scooby says and pokes his head out of a pile of Aztec treasure!

"Oh, no! Treasure!" Daphne moans.

"Like what's wrong with treasure, Daph?" Shaggy chuckles.

"Treasure means tomb robbers and booby-traps," Daphne replies. "We've got to get out of here."

"Great idea, but we're locked in a vault," Fred says.

Daphne looks around the chamber. If there's one thing she's learned, it's that this pyramid is full of trapdoors. She runs her hand along every bump and irregularity on the walls. Sure enough, a section of the wall slides open.

A hideous face stares out of the darkness!

Turn to page 88.

Shaggy sees a crowbar resting on a nearby crate. He reaches for it, but it's just beyond his grasp.

"If I could just get that crowbar I could pry open the cage door," he says.

A forklift rumbles toward them. It picks up the cage holding Fred, Daphne, and Velma and puts them in the back of a truck. They're being smuggled!

"Zoinks! We'll never see them again!" Shaggy moans.

Scooby gets a determined look on his face and presses his back end against the cage door. His tail wriggles out like a monkey's and wraps around the crowbar.

"Way to go, Scoob!" Shaggy praises as he takes the crowbar and springs the cage door.

But are they too late? The truck is driving away!

Turn to page 76.

"Like, are we glad to see you!" the tall figure says as he takes off his hideous mask. It's Shaggy. Scooby takes of his mask, too. "Xolotl captured us and Daph and the professor. But Scoobs and I used these disguises to escape and find help to rescue them!"

"Take us to them!" Fred says.

"You mean you want us to go back there?" Shaggy shivers.

"You're the only ones who know the way," Velma says. "Besides, Daphne has Scooby Snacks in her purse."

"Rhut are re raiting for?" Scooby says and leads the way.

Shaggy and Scooby lead their friends to a pyramid in the center of the underground city.

"Daphne and the Professor are inside," Shaggy says.

"How do we get in?" Fred asks.

Turn the page.

"There's a door right here," Shaggy says. He presses a carving. A secret door opens. Inside is a room with suits and masks like Shaggy's.

"Those look like the suits people wear when they work in sterile rooms," Velma observes.

They put on the suits and masks. The masks self-seal and oxygen flows.

"Uncle Cosmo's workers probably saw people wearing these outfits and thought they were monsters. No wonder they ran off," Velma says.

As soon as the suits seal, a laser passes over them and an inner door opens. They gasp at what they see. They are in a room filled with wall-to-wall electronics.

"This is a single, giant computer hard drive!" Velma realizes.

"Voice recognition confirmed. Velma Dinkley," a voice states.

"The computer knows you!" Fred says.

"Like, that's spooky!" Shaggy says.

Scooby whimpers.

"Voice recognition confirmed. Fred Jones, Norville Shaggy Rogers, and Scooby-Doo," the computer declares.

"Zoinks! The computer knows us!" Shaggy exclaims.

"And so do I, you meddling kids!" a human voice says.

They turn to see a man in a clear plastic sterile suit.

"Dr. Laslow Ostwald!" Velma gasps.

The others look blank. "Who?"

"He built that high-tech house of horrors," Velma explains. "What did you name it? Dari? Carrie?"

"SHARI!" Ostwald retorts. "But she's reprogrammed now. I call her MARI."

Turn the page.

"Reprogrammed to do what?" Velma asks.

"MARI stands for Modified Artificial Robotic Intelligence, and she can hack into any secure computer network in the world," Ostwald replies.

"You're data mining," Fred says.

"I'm data stealing and selling," Ostwald boasts.

"You won't get away with it, Ostwald," Fred declares.

"You can't stop me. MARI, destroy them!" Ostwald commands. Nothing happens.

"I'm unable to comply," the computer says in a faint voice. Then all the lights on the hard drive go out.

"Your hacking days are over, Ostwald," Velma says. Her sealed mask is off. "I realized that this is a sterile room because any contamination would harm the hard drive. So I broke containment and 'infected' the computer. I'm sorry, MARI."

"Nooo! You don't know what you've done!" Ostwald moans. "All my buyers will come after me to deliver what I can't deliver!"

"Don't worry, you'll be safe in a nice jail cell," Fred assures him. "But first, show us where you've got Daphne and Professor Dinkley!"

Defeated, Ostwald agrees. He says they're in another room in the pyramid.

"Another mystery solved! Another bad guy unmasked!" Fred says.

They leave the room, but Velma stays behind. She looks at the giant hard drive then starts working the various keyboard controls. The computer's main hard drive module pops out of the console. Velma takes it out of the console and looks at it.

"I'll save you, MARI. Just be a good girl this time!" Velma says.

THE END

The treasure wave sweeps them down another tunnel. It's a short trip. They all fly out of the pyramid like a gushing fountain.

Fred, Velma, Daphne, and Shaggy land wearing Aztec treasure from head to toe. They look around for Scooby.

"Scooby-Doo, where are you?" Shaggy calls.

Scooby pops up wearing the Xolotl mask. A dazed man crawls out of the pile next to Scooby.

"You meddling kids. Not again!" the man mutters in a daze.

Suddenly Professor Dinkley runs up to the gang.

"Kids! I was working on an isolated section of the pyramid and heard the commotion! Is everyone okay?" Dinkley says. He recognizes the dazed man as his partner on the dig. "Professor Stonehack!"

"Professor Stonehack! I recognize that name!" Fred realizes.

"You were stealing Aztec relics the last time we saw you," Daphne says.

"Still up to your old tricks," Velma observes.

"Yes! I dressed up as Xolotl to scare off Cosmo's workers," Stonehack confesses. "I didn't want anyone to know I was looting treasure from the pyramid. I made sure Cosmo was busy digging all by himself in an isolated portion of the site. And I almost got away with it, too."

Professor Dinkley thanks the gang for solving the mystery.

"What can I do to repay you?" Dinkley asks.

"Tell us where can we get some good enchiladas! All this mystery-solving has made me work up an appetite!" Shaggy says.

THE END

Shaggy and Scooby have no idea where they're going, and they don't dare look! They fall down a mineshaft like pebbles down a drainpipe. **BING! BANG! BONG!** When they finally come to a halt, they are in a dusty ore cart full of rocks.

"Ow! That was a harsh landing!" Shaggy groans.

Scooby and Shaggy finally open their eyes, but it's dark and they can't see much more than vague shadows.

"Well, at least there's no fire and brimstone," Shaggy says.

They climb out of the cart and start to walk along the tracks.

"Like, I don't know where we're going, but I hope it's somewhere safe!" Shaggy declares.

Suddenly a bright light shines in their eyes. It's moving toward them.

It's a train!

Shaggy and Scooby jump in alarm and their hair stands on end.

"R-r-run!" Scooby shouts.

They peel out, back the way they came, with legs spinning like racecar wheels. A couple of seconds later, a steam locomotive thunders over the spot where they were just standing. Shaggy and Scooby run as fast as they can, but the ore train gains on them.

"This is the end, pal!" Shaggy wails.

Suddenly they spot a pair of stalactites hanging over the tracks. They grab onto them and swing out of the train's path. The ore train passes under them. But the pals can't hang onto the slippery stones.

Turn the page.

"Ruh-roh!" Scooby gulps and drops into one of the ore carts being pulled by the train.

"I'm coming, buddy!" Shaggy shouts and lets go. He lands in another ore cart and runs to reach Scooby.

The train comes out of the dark tunnel and into a large, bright cave. There are several vats pouring out streams of molten metal.

"It's a smelting factory!" Shaggy realizes.

The ore train stops and begins to dump its load into empty vats. Suddenly the pals are tipped into one of the vats along with the raw ore.

The vat rumbles on a conveyor belt headed toward a huge furnace!

Turn to page 104.

Scooby and Shaggy try to climb out of the vat but it's too deep. That's when they see Fred, Velma, and Daphne below them!

"Help! Help! Up here!" Shaggy yells to his friends.

But the gang is being chased by Xolotl! They're yelling for help, too!

"Re'll save rou!" Scooby says. He and Shaggy throw chunks of ore at Xolotl.

One chunk bounces off Xolotl's dog head and knocks him down. Daphne looks up and sees Shaggy and Scooby. She reaches into her purse and pulls out a spool of dental floss. She ties one end to the chunk of ore and swings it like a bolo. The weighted dental floss wraps around a knob on the vat.

"Pull!" Daphne tells Fred and Velma.

The vat tips and Shaggy and Scooby fall out before it enters the blast furnace.

"That was close!" Shaggy says.

They run over to their friends and the fallen Xolotl, whose dog head looks a little crooked! Velma leans over and removes his mask. Everyone gasps.

"Dr. LaRue!" Velma says. "The last time we met, you tried to steal Montezuma's Mexican treasure!"

"I can't believe it! Mystery Inc. foiled me again," LaRue laments. "I found an old Aztec gold mine under Professor Dinkley's dig site and invented the Xolotl disguise to scare people away from my discovery."

"Where's Uncle Cosmo?" Velma wants to know.

"I sent him to a resort in Cancun. He's probably at the all-you-can-eat buffet right now," LaRue says.

"All you can eat?" Shaggy and Scooby say and hightail it out of the factory!

THE END

AUTHOR

Laurie S. Sutton has read comics since she was a kid. She grew up to become an editor for Marvel, DC Comics, Starblaze, and Tekno Comics. She has written Adam Strange for DC, Star Trek: Voyager for Marvel, plus Star Trek: Deep Space Nine and Witch Hunter for Malibu Comics. There are long boxes of comics in her closet where there should be clothing and shoes. Laurie has lived all over the world. She currently resides in Florida.

ILLUSTRATOR

Scott Neely has been a professional illustrator and designer for many years. Since 1999, he's been an official Scooby-Doo and Cartoon Network artist, working on such licensed properties as Dexter's Laboratory, Johnny Bravo, Courage The Cowardly Dog, Powerpuff Girls, and more. He has also worked on Pokémon, Mickey Mouse Clubhouse, My Friends Tigger & Pooh, Handy Manny, Strawberry Shortcake, Bratz, and many other popular characters. He lives in a suburb of Philadelphia and has a scrappy Yorkshire Terrier, Alfie.

GLOSSARY

albino (al-BYE-noh)—a person or animal born without any natural coloring in the skin, hair, or eyes

archeologist (ar-kee-OL-uh-jist)—a scientist who studies the past by digging up old buildings and objects and examining them carefully

chupacabra (CHOO-puh-kah-brah)—a mythical doglike creature said to live in parts of Mexico and Puerto Rico

contamination (kuhn-TAM-uh-nay-shun)—the act of making something dirty or unfit for use

conveyor belt (kuhn-VEY-ur BELT)—a moving belt that carries objects from one place to another in a factory

sarcophagus (sahr-KOF-uh-guhs)—a stone coffin

smelting (SMEL-ting)—melting ore so that the metal can be removed

stalagmite (stuh-LAG-mite)—a thin piece of rock shaped like an icicle that sticks up from the floor of a cave

subterranean (suhb-tuh-REY-nee-uhn)—underground

tsunami (tsoo-NAH-mee)—a very large, destructive wave caused by an underwater earthquake or volcano

Xolotl (szh-LOW-till)—Aztec god of fire and death

What did the mad scientist say when he stole the Aztec treasure?

a. "It's all Mayan!"

b. "This stuff must Cozumel-lion (cost a million) bucks!"

c. "A museum will peso much to get this back!"

What kind of insects bothered Scooby-Doo down in Mexico?

a. Az-ticks!

b. Mesquite-oes!

c. Not a lot of insects, just Juan.

Why did the sneaky crocodile follow Scooby through the jungle?

a. It was an "investi-gator"!

b. It was a "crept-tile"!

c. It was hungry for something crunchy and Scooby was acting like he was nuts!

How did Daphne know a mummy was following her?

a. She could hear it coffin.
b. She could hear it humming a tomb.
c. She could hear it rapping (wrapping).

How was Fred able to get inside the Aztec temple?

a. The temple was holy, so he crawled through a hole.
b. Fred is such a snappy dresser, no matter where he goes, he's "in."
c. He used Az-tech support.

Why did the Aztec ghost have a dog head?

a. So he could hound his enemies!
b. So he could strike terrier into people's hearts!
c. He wanted to make his enemies flea!

THE CHOICE IS YOURS!